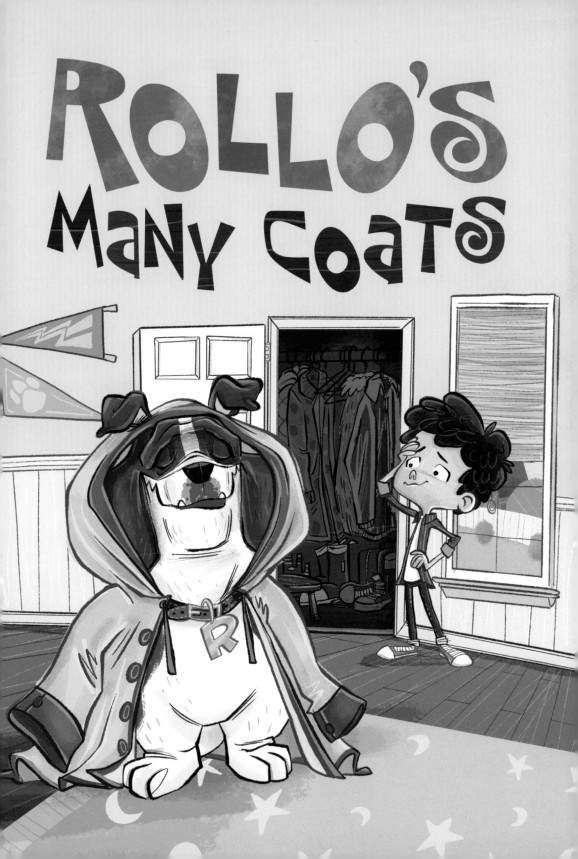

ABOUT THE AUTHOR:

Reed Duncan is an author as well as a former
reading instructor, teacher, and school administrator.
He lives in Vermont. The Rollo stories are based on
Reed and his real-life, rambunctious bulldog,
who has many, many coats.

W

PENGUIN WORKSHOP
An Imprint of Penguin Random House LLC, New York

Text copyright © 2020 by Reed Duncan. Illustrations copyright © 2020 by Penguin Random House LLC.
All rights reserved. Published by Penguin Workshop, an imprint of Penguin Random House LLC, New York.
PENGUIN and PENGUIN WORKSHOP are trademarks of Penguin Books Ltd, and the W colophon
is a registered trademark of Penguin Random House LLC. Manufactured in China.

Visit us online at www.penguinrandomhouse.com.

Library of Congress Cataloging-in-Publication Data is available upon request.

ISBN 9781524792497   10 9 8 7 6 5 4 3 2 1

ROLLO'S MANY COATS

by REED DUNCAN

illustrated by KEITH FRAWLEY

PENGUIN WORKSHOP

Rollo, are you ready for the party tonight?
We need to find your party coat.

You have all kinds of coats,
but only ONE party coat.

Let's look for it!

No, not that coat, Rollo.

That's a winter coat for when it is cold.
It's too heavy for a party.

Let's keep looking.

No, not that one, Rollo.

Your raincoat is for wet days.

No, not that coat, Rollo.

The furry coat is too fancy.
It is not the coat we are looking for.

No, Rollo.

Your checkered coat is a special coat,
but it is not your party coat.

No, not that coat, Rollo.
That's the hiding coat.

You don't want to hide
at tonight's party.

Will we ever find your party coat?

Let's keep looking.

No, we're not looking for your vest, Rollo.

It has no sleeves.
It is not a coat.

No, Rollo, we're not looking for
the walking coat,

or the reading coat,

or the eating coat.

None of these are your party coat.

Let's keep looking!

The pocket coat with all the pouches?

No. That is not the party coat, either.

The dancing coat means that it is time to go dancing!

But tonight's party is not a dancing party.

That is not the right coat, either.

Do you know what kind of party it will be tonight?

A birthday party!

Happy birthday, Rollo!